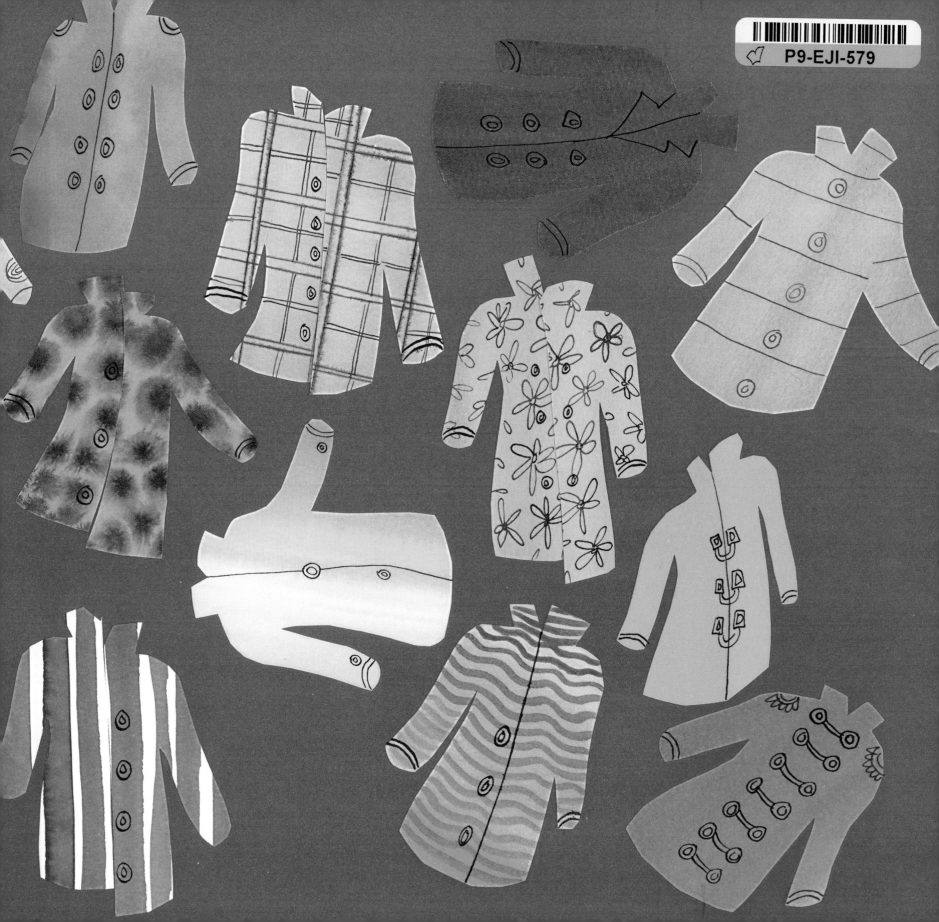

For Ellis and for Ton

MR. COATS

SIEB POSTHUMA   TRANSLATED BY DAVID COLMER

LQ
LEVINE QUERIDO

MONTCLAIR | AMSTERDAM | HOBOKEN

This is an Em Querido book • Published by Levine Querido

LEVINE QUERIDO

www.levinequerido.com · info@levinequerido.com

Levine Querido is distributed by Chronicle Books LLC

Library of Congress Control Number: 2021950063
ISBN 978-1-64614-184-5

Printed and bound in China

MIX
Paper from
responsible sources
FSC™ C104723

Published in August 2022
First Printing

Book design by Christine Kettner • The text type was set in Hightower

Sieb Posthuma created *Mr. Coats* when he was madly in love, as an ode to loving an equal spirit
who warms you from the inside out. Mr. Posthuma created the art for this book with cut outs,
Ecoline and black ink pens, and lots of love in his heart.

This publication has been made possible with
financial support from the Dutch Foundation for Literature.

Nederlands
letterenfonds
dutch foundation
for literature

ONCE UPON A TIME there was a little man who was always cold. He shivered autumn, winter, and spring, and even in summer when the sun was shining. He always stayed inside, close to his red-hot stoves.

He never had any visitors. His house was so boiling hot, no one else could stand it. Day and night he sat by himself with his teeth chattering. He didn't dare go outside—where it was even chillier.

One day, when the little man woke up freezing in bed yet again, he'd had enough. He pulled on three sets of thermal underwear, tied a hot water bottle onto his stomach, and put on three woolen sweaters, one over the other. Then he went into town, to the shops.

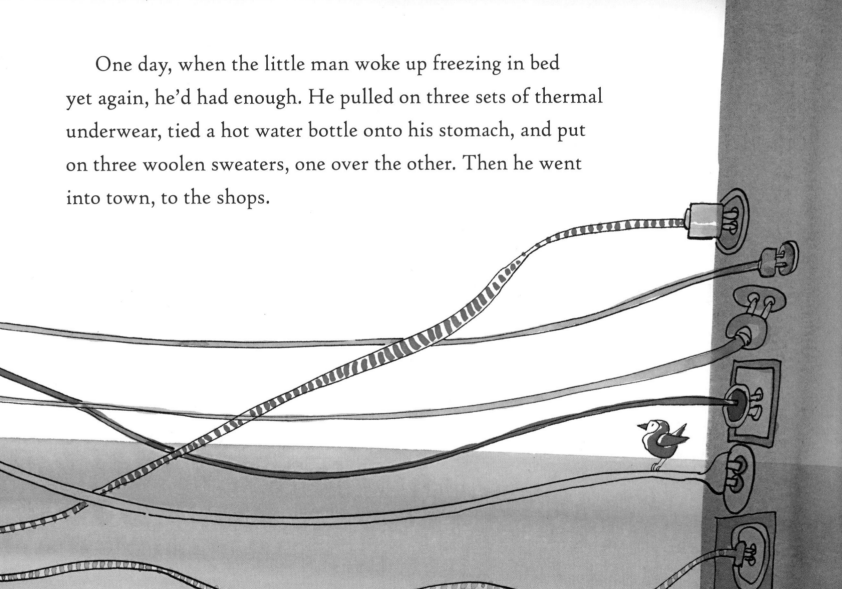

"I'm looking for a coat," the man said, shaking from the cold.
"The thickest one you have."

In no time he found just what he was looking for.

"I'll take three," he said, "and I'll put them all on right away."

But as soon as he left the store, he felt like he was back at the North Pole.

At the market he bought the warmest blankets he could find and asked a tailor to turn them into coats. He put all of those coats on too, over the ones he was already wearing.

On the street, everyone gaped. They had never seen anyone wear so many coats at once.

"Mr. Coats," the people shouted, "you're blue from the cold!"

The people went home to see if they had any old coats lying around. Mr. Coats put them all on but still felt chilled to the bone.

Shivering, he went back home. To his hot stoves and a nice pot of hot tea.

But when he tried to go inside, he got stuck in the doorway. With all those coats on, he didn't fit in his own house anymore!

Ice-cold tears rolled down his cheeks, and he pulled his head back into the collars of the coats.

Now his coats were his house. Mr. Coats lit a fire on the
ground between his coattails to warm himself up.
   When people saw his house of coats they stopped and stared.
A reporter even came to take photos. They put him on the front
page of the newspaper.

After that, even more people came to admire his house.

One day, one of them shouted, "Mr. Coats, there's something
very special in my hometown that I need to show you."

The man hoisted the house of coats up onto a truck and got on the highway.

The people in the other cars stared and stared. They had never seen someone move like this before.

"Close your eyes!" the man said when the truck finally stopped.

When Mr. Coats opened his eyes, he could hardly believe it. He was looking at another house of coats just like his.

"This is where Mrs. Coats lives," the man said. He grabbed one of the coat-house sleeves and shouted into the hole, "Mrs. Coats, visitors!"

A little later a head appeared, Mrs. Coats's head.
Her mouth fell open with surprise.

Mrs. Coats and Mr. Coats had a lot to talk about: electric blankets, hot water bottles, earmuffs, cups of hot chocolate, sun lamps, fur-lined boots...

Suddenly Mrs. Coats said, "It's funny, but I'm starting to warm up. I can feel a drop of perspiration on my forehead!"

"Now that you mention it," Mr. Coats said, "I don't feel as cold anymore either!"

And while they talked, they peeled off coat after coat.

After a couple of hours, they were only wearing two coats each, and their teeth had long stopped chattering.

"How do you like my house?" Mrs. Coats asked. "I couldn't get in through the door with all those coats on, but now I can."

"I feel right at home," said Mr. Coats.

Soon Mr. Coats got his things from his own house
and moved in with Mrs. Coats. Every day they spent
hours chatting on the bench close to the house. Hanging
on the coat rack were just two coats. His and hers.

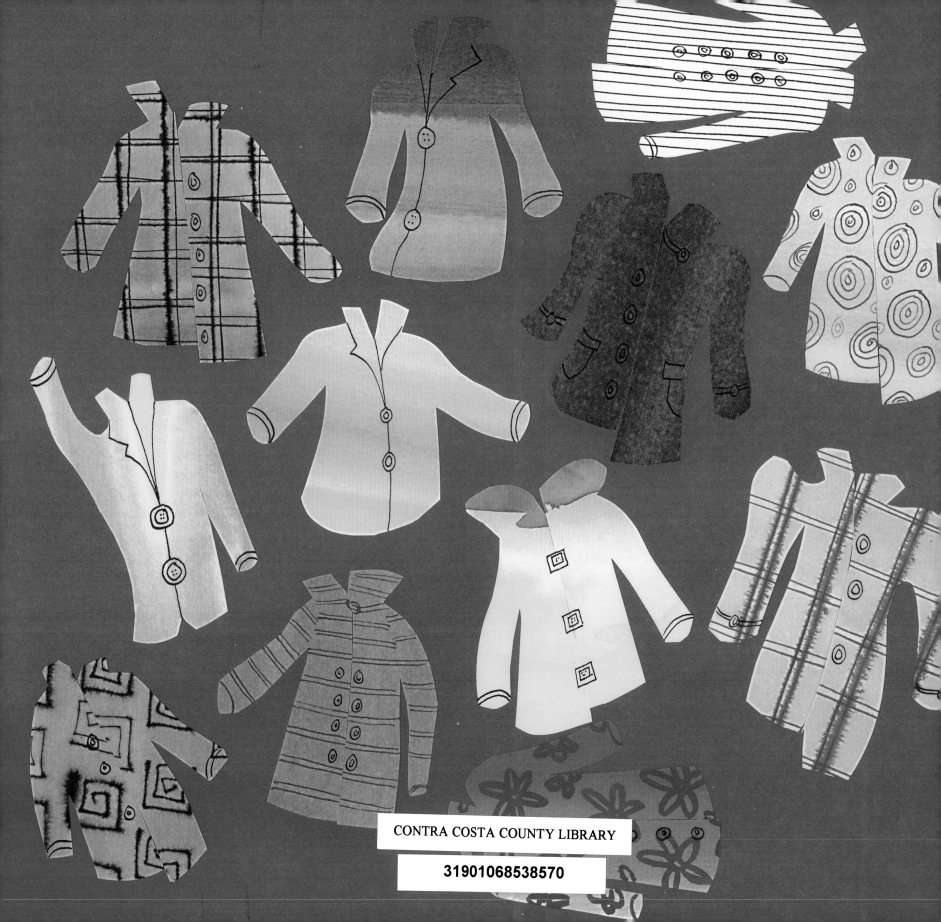